For Duncan Williamson, the great Scottish storyteller – E.M.

About the Story

The story comes from the Scottish travellers' tradition.
This version was told to Eric Maddern
by the traditional Scottish storyteller Duncan Williamson.

Death in a Nut copyright © Frances Lincoln Limited 2005
Text copyright © Eric Maddern 2005
Illustrations copyright © Paul Hess 2005

First published in Great Britain in 2005 by
Frances Lincoln Children's Books, 4 Torriano Mews, Torriano Avenue, London NW5 2RZ
www.franceslincoln.com

Distributed in the USA by Publishers Group West

All rights reserved

No part of this publication may be reproduced,
stored in a retrieval system, or transmitted, in any form, or by any means, electrical,
mechanical, photocopying, recording or otherwise without the prior
written permission of the publisher or a licence permitting restricted copying. In the United Kingdom
such licences are issued by the Copyright Licensing Agency, 90 Tottenham Court Road,
London W1P 9HE.

British Library Cataloguing in Publication Data available on request

ISBN 1-84507-081-X

Set in Avril

Printed in China

1 3 5 7 9 8 6 4 2

Death in a Nut

Retold by Eric Maddern

Illustrated by Paul Hess

FRANCES LINCOLN CHILDREN'S BOOKS

Once upon a time there was a lad called Jack who lived with his mother in a cottage by the sea. They kept hens, a goat and a vegetable garden. Jack's mother took in sewing, and that's how they got by.

What Jack loved best was walking along

the beach looking for things washed up

by the sea — old drums, rusty chains, fishing-nets

and driftwood for his mother's fire.

Early one morning Jack knocked on his mother's door with a cup of tea. There was no answer, so he peeped inside. She was lying pale and still.

"What's the matter, Mother?" asked Jack.

"I'm so poorly, dear boy," she wheezed. "I think Old Man Death will be coming for me soon!"

"No, Mother," said Jack. "Please don't die. I've got no one in the world but you."

"Hush now, Jack," she said. "You're young. You've got plenty of life ahead of you. You'll get married and have a family. Now let me rest a while."

Jack went down to the beach thinking about his poor mother.

Suddenly he saw an old man walking towards him with a ragged black coat, deep sunken eyes and a scythe that glinted in the morning sunshine. Jack knew it was the Grim Reaper, Old Man Death himself.

The old man greeted Jack politely, asking how far it was to the next cottage.

"That's my mother's cottage," said Jack. "You're not going there!"

"Well, she's ill and in pain," said Death.

"It's natural, you know.

It's time for her to go."

"No!" cried Jack.

"You're not taking my mother!"

And he leapt on the old man, snatched his scythe and smashed it on the rocks.

"Young man, you've done it now," said Death, and the two of them piled into each other. But strangely, every time Jack punched Death, the old man got smaller and smaller, until at last Jack had him in the palm of his hand.

Then he found a hazelnut with a hole where a squirrel had taken the nut. He squeezed Old Man Death head first into the hole and plugged it with a stick.

There he had him: Death in a Nut!

Jack leaned back and threw the nut far out, SPLOSH, into the salty water. "He'll not be bothering my mother now — or anybody else, for that matter."

Jack smiled, and walked home

with a skip in his step.

His mother was in the kitchen making scones.

"But Mother," he said, "I thought you weren't feeling well."

"I wasn't," she said, "but just now a breeze blew away all my aches and pains and I'm better than I've felt for a long time. So why don't you fetch some eggs for our breakfast?"

Jack didn't say anything about Old Man Death. He went out to the hen house and found some big brown eggs.

In the kitchen, his mother was melting fat in the frying pan. She took an egg and cracked it on the side of the pan. CLUNK! It wouldn't break. She tried another — CLUNK!

"Strange," she said. "These eggs have gone right off. You'd better bring some leeks, carrots and turnips from the garden and I'll make soup for your dinner."

Jack brought in the vegetables, but every time his mother tried to chop them, the knife skidded straight off.

"How peculiar," she said. "They seem to be frozen solid."

"But we haven't had a frost for days," said Jack.

"Well, you'll have to kill the cockerel," she said. "We'll have him for our dinner instead."

Jack went out and grabbed the cockerel by its legs. He tucked it under his arm and tried to wring its neck. But every time, the neck — well, it unwrung itself.

He swung it round his head and bashed it against the wall, but still he couldn't kill that bird.

So he went in and said, "Mother, I can't do it."

"What's the matter?" she said. "Give it to me." She laid the cockerel on the block and chopped off its head. The head flew off... and then flew back on its shoulders again! Every time she chopped it off, the head jumped straight back on again.

When Jack arrived in the village there was a noisy crowd in the square, but Jack went straight to the butcher: "Could I have a couple of chops, please?"

"There'll be no chops today, my lad," said the butcher. "I tried to kill a bullock this morning, but every time it jumped back up on its feet again."

"We tried to kill a cockerel and the same thing happened," said Jack.

"You tried to kill one. I tried to kill ten. And it's happening everywhere. It's almost as if nothing will die any more!"

Then Jack realised.

It was something HE had done!

He ran all the way home and told his mother the whole story: how he'd met Death and squeezed him into a nut and flung him into the waves.

"Oh Jack!" she said. "You shouldn't have done that. We need Death to survive, my boy. You'd better go and find that nut!"

So Jack went to the beach and walked miles looking for the nut. After three days of searching he was hungry and tired.

Finally, he sat down by the water's edge and moaned, "What have I done to the world?"

Suddenly he saw, bobbing on the waves, a hazelnut with a stick poking out.

Jack had never been so pleased! He reached out, picked up the nut and pulled out the plug. Out popped a little head.

Old Man Death came from the nut and grew to his full size, with his ragged coat and deep sunken eyes.

"Aha!" he croaked. "You thought by getting rid of me, you'd stop all the troubles in the world! But without me, my boy, there can be no life."

"Now, Jack," he said, "You broke my scythe."

"My mother made me mend it. It's up in the porch."

Jack led Death to the cottage and handed him the scythe.
The old man tested the edge of the blade with his thumb.
"You've done a good job, Jack," he said.
"And because you've been fair to me,
I'll leave your mother for a while."

Then he stepped off the porch and disappeared.

After that, Jack's mother lived to a ripe old age.

And when Old Man Death finally came for her Jack didn't mind, because now he knew

that without Death there can be no Life.